Mermaid School

Secrets of the Palace

Mermaid School

The Clamshell Show

Ready, Steady, Swim!

Secrets of the Palace

Mermaid School

Secrets of the Palace

Written by
Lucy Courtenay
Illustrated by Sheena Dempsey

Amulet Books
New York

PUBLISHER'S NOTE: This is a work of fiction. Names, characters, places, and incidents are either the product of the author's imagination or used fictitiously, and any resemblance to actual persons, living or dead, business establishments, events, or locales is entirely coincidental.

Cataloging-in-Publication Data has been applied for and may be obtained from the Library of Congress.

Hardcover ISBN 978-1-4197-4524-9
Paperback ISBN 978-1-4197-4525-6

Printed and bound in U.S.A.
10 9 8 7 6 5 4 3 2 1

ABRAMS The Art of Books
195 Broadway, New York, NY 10007
abramsbooks.com

For Jess, with love.
L.C.
For
Marua A,
S.D.

Pearl's House

Galloping Scallop Café

Lord Foam's Atoll Academy

Mermaid Lagoon

(Not to scale

School Rock

To QUEEN MARETTA'S PALACE

Lady Sealia Foam's Mermaid School

Radio Seawave

Marnie's House

N
W
E
S
East Lagoon Rocks
Coral Ridge
Clamshell Grotto
"Christabel Loves Arthur" Rock
Orla's House

Marnie Blue stared at her plate.

"Mom?" she said cautiously. "What *is* it?"

Her mom wiped a blob of green gravy off the end of her nose. "Algae curry," she said. "It's *full* of vitamins."

Marnie prodded the dark green stew with her driftwood fork. The fork snapped in half. "It's full of sand too."

"The sand will help you to digest the curry," her mom explained. She sat down at the table in the middle of their little mermaid cave. "I was reading all about it in the recipe section of *Fishtales Monthly*. We should all have more sand in our diets."

Marnie put down her broken fork. "I think I'll wait for Aunt Christabel," she said. "Where is she anyway?"

"I have no idea," her mom admitted. "You know what your aunt is like with her galas and fashion shows and music awards. She'll turn up. Eat up before it gets cold!"

"It's already cold," Marnie pointed out.

"Well, eat up. We have a big day tomorrow and we're going to need all the energy we can get!"

Marnie cheered up a bit. Tomorrow was her first school field trip! The first years at Lady Sealia Foam's Mermaid School were going to Queen Maretta's Palace. Her mom had filled in all the forms and paid for Marnie's ticket. She had even volunteered to come along and help. Marnie was looking forward to it more than anything. She hoped she'd be in a group with her two best friends, Pearl Cockle and Orla Finnegan.

She looked out of the window at Mermaid Lagoon. There was no sign of Christabel's blue sea-moss coat, or her aunt's goldfish, Garbo, on her crystal-studded leash. It was very unlike her aunt to be late for dinner. Maybe Christabel was visiting her human boyfriend, Arthur.

Christabel was in a LOT of trouble because of Arthur. Humans weren't allowed in Mermaid Lagoon. *But what could you do*, Marnie wondered, *when it was true love?* Christabel had sparkly crystal tears in a bowl, and *everyone* knew you only cried crystal tears when it was true love.

Marnie thought about the wish she had recently made for her aunt's happiness. Queen Maretta herself had magically appeared and granted the wish. Maybe Christabel and Arthur were secretly getting married right now!

"Horace?" her mom said, waking Marnie from her daydream. "Light."

The large anglerfish above the kitchen table switched on his light. The rocky cave filled with a cozy glow.

"So!" her mom said. "Queen Maretta's Palace! I went there on a school trip when I was your age too. It is the most beautiful building in the whole lagoon." She took a large scoop of algae curry and put it in her mouth. She chewed and swallowed, making a face.

The palace was a long way away. Marnie hoped she wouldn't be sick on the journey. She certainly *would* be sick if she ate this algae.

"I want to see the Jewel Room, with the famous Ocean Orb of Truth," she said aloud as she pushed her curry around her plate. "Queen Maretta used it to see the truth about the war with the storm sprites—that storms were good for the lagoon's ecology—and saved the merfolk from any more battles! But I'm not sure I'd be brave enough to look in the Orb. Apparently it shows you the truth about every bad thing you've ever done as well. Oh! And can I please have some sand dollars for the gift shop?"

The door to the cave burst open. Christabel Blue, star of the *Big Blue Show* and the most famous mermaid in Mermaid Lagoon, swam inside.

"Sorry I'm late," Christabel said. Horace's light reflected off her huge crystal necklace and bounced little swirls of brightness off the rocky walls. "The traffic was terrible. Have you ever tried swimming through a school of tunafish?" She frowned and sniffed. "What *is* that smell?"

She took off her sea-moss coat and hung it on a barnacle hook by the door. Then she unclipped Garbo's leash, and Garbo immediately swam off into the other room.

"I'm glad you could make it, Christabel," her mom said. "We thought you might miss dinner."

"You didn't answer my question," said Christabel. She gave Marnie a big lipsticky kiss on the top of her head. "It smells like King Neptune's armpits in here."

"It's algae and sand curry," Marnie explained.

"Yuck!" Christabel said. "Let's get takeout instead. I know a charming octopus who does marvelous things with seaweed noodles. I'll send him a scallop right away."

She dug around in her pearl-studded handbag and pulled out a dainty little scallop. Tucking a note into the scallop's beautiful fan-shaped shell, Christabel opened the door again and sent the scallop on its way.

Her mom defiantly ate more of the green sludge. "It's delicious," she said. "And very good for you!"

As her aunt settled down at the table, Marnie thought she looked a bit distracted. She darted little glances at Christabel over her broken driftwood fork.

"Where have you been, Aunt Christabel?" she asked at last, as her mom scraped up the last fronds of algae from her plate.

"Here and there," said Christabel vaguely. "What are you up to tomorrow, darlings?"

"We're going to Queen Maretta's Palace," Marnie explained. "Everyone says it's got an *amazing* gift shop."

"But we're not going for the gift shop," said Marnie's mom. She took another brave bite of curry. "We're going for the history! The architecture! The experience!"

"Do you remember our school trip there, Daffy?" Christabel asked. "We had a lot of fun in the air fountain. If you put your mouth on an air jet," she told Marnie, "you can do the most amazing burps."

Marnie's mom sighed. "Honestly Christabel, you are *terrible*."

"What can I say?" said Christabel. She gave a faint smile. "I live life to the fullest."

"Why don't you come with us, Aunt Christabel?" Marnie asked.

Christabel waved a hand. Her rings glittered in Horace's light. "School trips aren't really my thing, darling," she said. "Ah, here is the octopus with our noodles already. Didn't I tell you he was *marvelous*?"

Chapter Two

Marnie woke up with a flip-flopping feeling of excitement, as if there was a fish in her tummy trying to get out. Today was the day she would see Queen Maretta's Palace with its gleaming crystal windows and famous coral gardens and incredible gift shop! She hurried to the bathroom to wash her face and scrub her tail with a sea sponge until it gleamed. Then she put on her school uniform, brushed her hair fifty times—she was too excited to do the full one hundred today—tied it up with a pearl bobble, and swam into the kitchen.

Everything was dark.

"Mom?" Marnie said, peering around in the gloom. "Horace?"

Horace floated sleepily out of his hole in the ceiling and switched on his light. Marnie gazed at the empty breakfast table.

"Mom!" she shouted. "We're going to be late!"

A terrible groaning sound came from her mom's bedroom. Marnie swam down the corridor. Horace followed with his swinging light.

"Is everything all right?" Marnie asked, poking her head around the door.

Her mom was lying in bed. Her face was the same color as last night's curry. "Not . . . feeling well," she croaked.

Panic gripped Marnie. "But we've got the school trip!"

Marnie's mom groaned again. There was a sound, followed by a nasty smell. A cluster of greenish bubbles rose to the rocky ceiling of the cave. "I'm sorry, darling," she gasped. "But I really don't think . . . Urgh . . ."

Christabel appeared at the door, yawning and patting her hair.

"Aunt Christabel, what's the matter with Mom?" Marnie asked.

"Algae and sand curry," said Christabel, wrinkling her nose. "Daffy, you poor thing. I always said that health food was bad for you."

"I feel awful," Marnie's mom said.

"You smell awful too," said Christabel. "Let's open a window. A few squirts of perfume wouldn't hurt either."

Marnie felt anxious. "But . . . what about my trip?"

Marnie's mom propped herself up in bed. Her eyes were bloodshot and bleary. "I'm so sorry, Marnie," she said. "But I can't go like this."

"*You* didn't eat the stuff, darling," Christabel said, putting a comforting arm around Marnie's shoulders. "So you can still go to the palace."

Tears sprang to Marnie's eyes. "But it was going to be really fun with Mom," she said. "And we were . . . we were going to go together . . ."

"There, there," Christabel said as Marnie burst into tears. "Perhaps I could come instead? I know I'm not your mother, but I've heard that I can be quite fun sometimes."

Marnie wiped her eyes. "But you said school trips weren't your thing."

"But my niece very much IS my thing," said Christabel. "And we can't have you in tears. Crying makes your skin blotchy."

Marnie threw her arms around her aunt. "Thank you!" she said. "But are you sure you won't be missing something important? You have your radio show and all your work."

Marnie's mom farted again, extremely loudly. Horace backed out of the room.

"What can be more important than escaping this terrible smell?" Christabel said. "I'll send a scallop to the studio and postpone today's recording. Daffy darling, will you be OK by yourself?"

Marnie's mom waved a hand weakly. "I'll be fine," she said. "Take some sand dollars from the clam in the kitchen for the gift shop, Marnie. Don't forget to appreciate the architecture . . . urgh . . ."

They left the bedroom, and Christabel gently shut the door. "I'd better get ready then," she said.

Marnie glanced at the starfish clock in the kitchen. "We're supposed to be at school at quarter past the morning starfish," she said. "It's already quarter to."

Christabel swam back to her bedroom. "Plenty of time! Go and have some breakfast. I'll be out in a tick."

Marnie helped herself to a bowl of Coral Crunch. She brushed her teeth. She took her packed lunch out of the cold-cave box—three seaweed wraps, a bottle of algae juice, and a packet of sea-cucumber slices—and slid it into her lunchbox. She tickled the kitchen clam so it opened its shell and let her take out two sand dollars. She carried a warm drink to her mom and kissed her goodbye. Then she sat down on a stool and waited for her aunt.

As the starfish clock arms moved to the top, Christabel swam out of her room. She looked exactly the same as when she had swum INTO her room.

"Aren't you dressed yet?" Marnie said.

"I have everything under control," said Christabel. "Have you seen my sea-mud face cream?"

"No. But Aunt Christabel . . ." Marnie began.

Christabel swam into the bathroom and shut the door. Marnie tidied the kitchen to take her mind off the time. Maybe she should just go without her aunt. It was getting late. Lady Sealia was very strict about punctuality.

Christabel finally sailed out of the bathroom as the starfish clock arms edged toward five past. Her hair and make-up were perfect, but she was still in her sea-moss bathrobe. "I'm almost ready! Just one or two more things," she said.

"Like clothes?" said Marnie.

Christabel wagged her finger. "I just need a teensy bit more time to find my favorite sea-silk jacket."

"They're going to leave without us!" Marnie shouted as Christabel vanished back into her bedroom.

"It's so important to present a stylish face to my fans," Christabel shouted back. "I can't go out looking anything but my best."

At ten past the starfish, Christabel drifted back into the hall, patted her hair in the hallway crystal mirror, attached an enormous pair of coral earrings, clipped Garbo on to her lead, scooped up her pearl-studded handbag, and struck a pose.

"How do I look?" she said.

"You look VERY LATE!" Marnie said.

"I'll just send a quick scallop to the radio station," said Christabel, digging through her bag.

"Can you do that on the way?" Marnie pleaded.

The lagoon was busy with early-morning traffic. A shoal of groupers was causing a bottleneck, and the water was thick with impatient tails. Messenger scallops flashed through the glittering water. Marnie dodged through the crowds, dragging Christabel with her.

"It's Christabel Blue!" squealed a dark-haired merman with three tigerfish. "Christabel, I *adore* you. Can I have your autograph?"

"Well of course—" Christabel began.

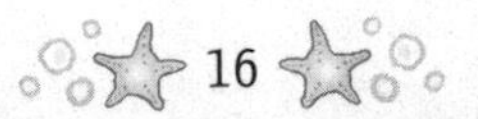

“Sorry,” said Marnie firmly, seizing her aunt’s hand. “Not today. We’re in a hurry!”

School Rock finally came into view. Marnie swam hard, pulling Christabel with her. She could see her whole class floating around a huge whale shark near the main entrance to the school.

An octopus in glasses was frowning in her direction.

“Late, Marnie Blue!” Miss Tangle said. “Typical!”

Chapter Three

"Sorry, Miss Tangle!" Marnie panted, clutching her side. "We swam as fast as we could."

There was a rush of excited chatter among the first years as they recognized Marnie's aunt.

"Christabel!" squeaked Mabel Anemone. "You're my favorite singer in the whole ocean!"

Marnie rolled her eyes. It was so *weird* how everyone freaked out about Christabel all the time.

Miss Tangle folded her eight arms. She looked suspiciously at Christabel. "I thought your mother was joining us, Marnie?" she said. Miss Tangle was **NOT** a fan of Christabel Blue.

There was a glint in Christabel's eye. She didn't like Miss Tangle much either. "Daffy has a bad case of the bubblers, Miss Tangle, so I've come instead."

Miss Tangle looked confused. "The bubblers?"

"Oh, she's not feeling well," explained Christabel sweetly. "She ate some bad algae, so she's got the booty belches."

Miss Tangle looked horrified. The first years burst out laughing. Gilly whispered something in Mabel's ear, then waved her hand in front of her nose, smirking.

Marnie blushed bright red. It wasn't difficult to guess what Gilly was whispering about. Marnie's best friends Pearl and Orla smiled at her sympathetically.

Mr. Scampi, the oceanography teacher, and Lady Sealia were also joining the trip. Lady Sealia sat in the front seat of her seashell carriage with her dogfish, Dilys, asleep on the seat beside her, tapping her fingers on the carriage windowsill. Typhoon the seahorse snorted and grumbled in the carriage harness. Mr. Scampi clacked his lobster claws together and bowed to Christabel.

"Always a delight, Miss Blue," he said, twirling his moustache.

"You're such a darling," said Christabel. She glanced at the whale shark. "Are we really traveling on this old thing?"

The school whale shark was old and a bit hard of hearing. His chin was resting on the lagoon bed and he was snoring gently, making the water ripple.

"Yes," snapped Miss Tangle. "He seats twenty-nine very comfortably."

"The seashell carriage would be better," said Christabel, waving at Lady Sealia's carriage. "I gave up public transport years ago."

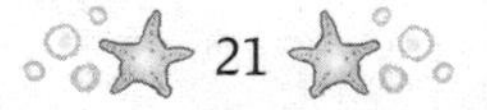

Gilly whispered something else to Mabel. Marnie stared at her tail, feeling awkward. It was easy to forget how much of a diva her aunt could be sometimes.

"We'll be in six groups of five: four students and one adult," Miss Tangle said, ignoring Christabel. "Please listen for your names and join the adult in charge of your group. You must stay with your group AT ALL TIMES. Ellie Plankton, Hali Fysshe-Fynne, Kerri Kelp-Matthews, and Salmonella Stone—you will be with Mr. Kelp-Matthews."

Kerri Kelp-Matthews's dad was a cheery looking merman with a big orange beard. He had come as one of the parent volunteers. His group clustered around him.

"Mabel Anemone, Marnie Blue, Pearl Cockle, and Orla Finnegan will be with Miss Blue," Miss Tangle continued.

Marnie beamed as Pearl and Orla swam over. The trip wouldn't be the same if she wasn't with her two best friends. Mabel gave a squeal of excitement and started swimming towards Christabel too.

Gilly grabbed Mabel's arm. "Mabel's going to be in *my* group, Miss Tangle," she said. "Aren't you, Mabel?"

Mabel looked unhappy, but stayed where she was.

"Lupita Barracuda, Allira Bladder, Treasure Jones, and Mintie Spratt will be with me," Miss Tangle went on.

Gilly tossed her curly blonde hair. "Miss Tangle! Make sure I'm with MABEL."

Miss Tangle ignored Gilly. "Dora Agua, Fresca Brooke, Ripley van der Zee, and Kenda Wells, you will be with Mr. Scampi. Nerida Attwater, Salina Fysshe-Fynne, Cordelia Glitter, and Gilly Seaflower will be supervised by Lady Sealia."

Lady Sealia gave a queenly wave from the carriage. Typhoon snorted in his harness and kicked hard with his bony tail. No one dared to ride or even *pat* Typhoon, but he made an excellent carriage seahorse when he was in the right mood. Which wasn't often.

"I can't wait!" said Pearl, pushing her glasses up her nose. "Everyone says Queen Maretta's ultra-rare fish collection is off the REEF."

"Who cares about fish when there's a gift shop?" said Orla. She linked arms with Marnie. "This is going to be SO cool."

"And finally," said Miss Tangle, "Jaya Wetson, Finnula Gritt, Marina Bailey, and Zarya Sand-Smith will be with Dr. Wetson."

Marnie could hardly see Jaya Wetson's mother

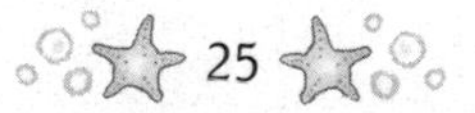

through the swarm of scallops that surrounded her. Several scallops were snapping their shells at Dr. Wetson's nose, trying to get her attention. Others were flapping away, clutching important messages in their shells.

"But I wanted to be with Mabel," Gilly insisted.

Miss Tangle peered at Gilly over her spectacles. "Mabel is with Miss Blue and you are with Lady Sealia, Gilly," she said. "There will be no changes. We simply don't have time."

"And we all know whose fault THAT is," said Gilly, glaring at Marnie.

Marnie bit her lip. Gilly was always picking on her.

The first years swam aboard the whale shark and settled down on his spotty back.

Gilly grabbed Mabel's hand.

"Miss Tangle said I had to stay with my group," Mabel said.

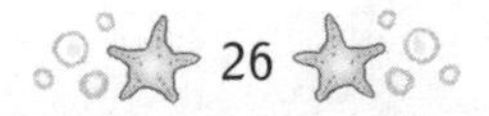

"You can sit with me on the whale shark though," Gilly said. "The best seats are always at the back. Come on. Before the *losers* get them." She shot another mean look at Marnie and dragged Mabel down to the whale shark's tail.

Marnie dipped her head and concentrated on fastening her seaweed seatbelt.

Christabel was still lingering beside Lady Sealia's seashell carriage. "I could squeeze into the carriage with you, Lady Sealia," she suggested. Garbo teased Typhoon, darting around him. The grumpy seahorse lashed his tail. "I'm sure Dilys won't mind sitting on your lap."

"Come along, Miss Blue," Miss Tangle said, tapping several of the starfish watches that she wore on her tentacles. "All aboard."

The gleam was back in Christabel's eyes. "Very well," she said. "Goodbye Typhoon, darling. Be good and FAST for Lady Sealia, won't you?"

Then she gave Typhoon a cheery pat on the neck.

No one touched Typhoon. NO ONE. His eyes bulged. His fins bristled. He roared with fury. And then he took off, the seashell carriage bumping and flying along behind him. The sound of Lady Sealia's screams drifted on the current. Then they were gone.

Chapter Four

"Do you think Lady Sealia is there already?" Pearl asked.

"She probably got there hours ago," said Orla. "If Typhoon swam that fast the whole way."

The whale shark lumbered along the seabed, keeping his mouth wide open for krill. Gilly and Mabel were the only mermaids sitting at the back. They were both looking a bit green as the whale shark swished his tail around.

Most of Marnie's class had already opened their packed lunches to snack. Kelp fritters, seaweed rolls, and sea-cucumber slices were swapped. Sea-anemone juice was traded for fizzy whelks and minnow chews. Garbo was swimming up and down, scrounging for snacks. Everyone was telling jokes to help pass the time.

"What do you call a mermaid that swims really fast?" Orla asked. "A blurmaid!"

"What did the shark say when he ate the clownfish?" Pearl returned. "'This tastes funny.'"

"What do you call this sandwich?" said Christabel.

"I don't know," said Marnie with interest. "What **DO** you call this sandwich?"

"It's not a joke, darling," said Christabel. She was holding one of Marnie's sandwiches between two fingers. "I am curious to know the answer."

"It's a seaweed wrap," said Marnie, taking it back. "It's my favorite."

"A seaweed wrap is a beauty treatment," said Christabel. "Not a sandwich." Opening her handbag, she pulled out a pretty packet of sugar-kelp cookies and nibbled on them.

"I feel sick, Miss Tangle," moaned Mabel, still sitting on the whale shark's swishing tail.

"Move up then, you silly girl!" said Miss Tangle.

Mabel swam up the whale shark's back and sat down with Marnie's group. Gilly folded her arms and looked furious.

"Sugar-kelp cookie?" Christabel said, offering Mabel a cookie.

"Thank you," whispered Mabel. "Can you sign it please?"

Christabel looked surprised. "You want me to sign a cookie?"

"You're right. Maybe I'll just keep it," Mabel said adoringly. "With my special things."

"Waste of a good cookie," said Orla, swiping it from Mabel and crunching it up.

Miss Tangle clapped her tentacles. "Let's have a sing along!" she said.

The mermaids groaned.

"How about 'Ten Green Shipwrecks'?" suggested the octopus teacher brightly.

"*Ten green shipwrecks broken on the rocks,*

OH, ten green shipwrecks broken on the rocks . . ."

"I love your music so much, Christabel," Mabel stammered. "I'd like to be a singer when I'm older."

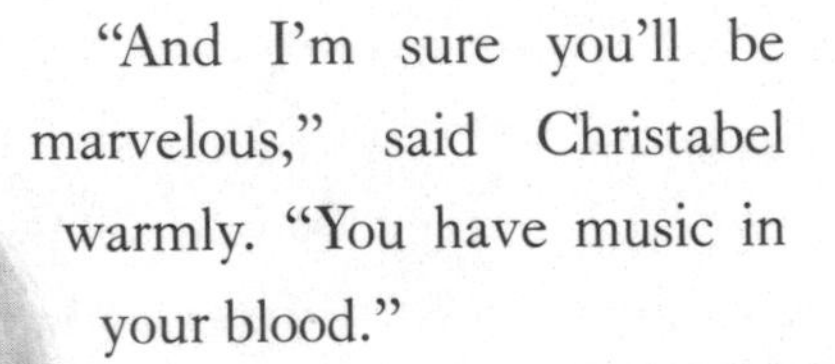

"And I'm sure you'll be marvelous," said Christabel warmly. "You have music in your blood."

"How can you tell?" Mabel said in amazement.

"The signs are all there, darling." Christabel patted Mabel's hand. "There is music in your speaking voice."

Mabel beamed. "My grandma was a singer. I hope one day I'll be just as good as her."

"Will you sing us a song, Christabel?" Dora asked.

"Yes!" Mabel gasped. "Sing 'Clamshell Heart'!"

"Sing 'Wave Goodbye'!"

"Of course I'll sing," Christabel said. "How about my latest single, 'It's Cod to Be You'?"

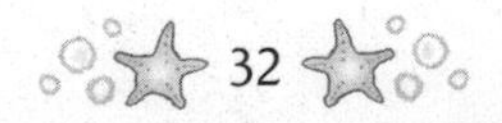

"Ooh!" the mermaids sighed. "It's Cod to Be You" had been all over Radio SeaWave for weeks. Everyone knew the words and the catchy tune.

"*And if one green shipwreck is towed back to the docks*," Miss Tangle was still singing loudly. "*There'll be EIGHT GREEN SHIPWRECKS BROKEN ON THE ROCKS.* Come along now!"

"*Eight-a green-a sheepwrecks, broken on the rocks*," sang Mr. Scampi dutifully. He had a strong accent when he sang, and was a little flat.

"*It's cod to be you, ooh, ooh, it's cod to be you*," Christabel sang, in her distinctive husky voice. "*Out here in the sea, just leave it to me, it's cod to be you . . .*"

Everyone swayed to the tune. Mr. Scampi stopped singing "Ten Green Shipwrecks" and waved his lobster claws above his head. Dr. Wetson scooped up all the messenger scallops that had followed her from School Rock, tucked them into her clamshell briefcase and joined in.

Still sitting by herself at the back of the whale shark, Gilly looked like a bad-tempered barracuda.

"You're really good," Mr. Kelp-Matthews told Christabel. "Have you thought about a singing career?" Miss Tangle made it to five green shipwrecks before she gave up. Marnie felt a little sorry for her teacher, but then Christabel moved on to the timeless classic, "In It to Fin It." Then she forgot about everything except the music.

"I can see it!" Pearl shouted. "I can see the palace!"

The coral walls and towers and courtyards of Queen Maretta's palace were peeping over the horizon. A thousand crystal windows glittered like underwater moonbeams. An impossible number of glimmering shells decorated the walls. Marnie couldn't believe how colorful it was. It was if a whole rainbow had fallen into the sea.

The mermaids all rushed out of their seats and gathered on the whale shark's nose to stare at the view.

"I read that the whole palace grew out of the seabed one stormy night," said Hali Fysshe-Fynne.

"That's a load of fishrot," said Hali's twin sister, Salina. "It grew out of a pearl that King Neptune dropped."

"Did not, barnacle brain," said Hali.

"Did too," said Salina. "And YOU'RE the barnacle brain."

"Back in your seats, everyone!" said Miss Tangle.

"The official history of the palace is unknown, but we do know that it has been here for over a hundred years. Queen Maretta herself is long gone, of course, although she makes an occasional magical appearance."

The other mermaids looked at Marnie, who blushed. Everyone knew she'd met the fabled mermaid queen herself, not so long ago.

The whale shark suddenly sneezed from the weight on its nose. Mintie Spratt fell off.

"This trip is amazing and we haven't even gotten there yet," Mabel said happily as they pulled Mintie out of a clump of red weed.

Up close, the palace was even more extraordinary. Marnie stared at the great air fountain, which spurted and bubbled and fizzed, and at all the mermaid tourists gathering in the enormous courtyard in front of the huge coral doors.

"Oh! I forgot my medicine today," said Pearl anxiously. She was allergic to coral.

A furious Lady Sealia was sitting on the edge of the air fountain. Dilys hung around her neck like a limp eel. Typhoon and the carriage were nowhere to be seen.

"You're late," Lady Sealia said as the mermaids climbed off the whale shark.

"I think maybe you were early, Lady Sealia," said Christabel.

Lady Sealia gave Christabel with the sort of look that would melt an iceberg from the bottom up. "Poor Dilys is feeling *quite* unwell," she said.

"Maybe it was something she ate," Christabel suggested. She swept her sea-moss scarf around her neck and waved at someone behind Lady Sealia. "Barbela, darling! How marvelous to see you!"

Barbela was one of the palace guards and one of the largest, strongest mermaids Marnie had ever seen. Her muscles were like rocks. She was wearing a magnificent uniform encrusted with pearls and carrying a very large trident.

"Christabel Blue!" Barbela said. "What an HONOR to have you at the palace today!"

Merfolk started to gather, having noticed Christabel. They pressed and pushed, trying to get as close as they could.

"Can I have a shellfie, Christabel?"

"I love your jacket!"

Christabel struck a few poses, waving and smiling. Marnie and her friends were jostled about by the crowd. Someone fell into the air fountain, and was whooshed straight up on a jet of bubbles. It was all a little scary.

"Stand BACK," bellowed Barbela. "Keep your distance from Miss Blue, please!"

The crowd melted away at the sight of Barbela's trident. A few merpeople hung around, staring and whispering. But Barbela glared, and soon they drifted off as well.

"What a lot of unnecessary excitement," said Lady Sealia.

"Thank you Barbela," Christabel said, straightening her sea-silk jacket. "You're an angelfish."

"Always at your service, Miss Blue," said Barbela.

Miss Tangle had turned purple with irritation. "Time for lunch," she said. "Unless Miss Blue has other ideas more suitable for *famous mermaids*."

Christabel put on her sunglasses. "Now that you mention it, Miss Tangle," she said, "I'm going to take my group for lunch in the palace restaurant. It will be more private there. I'm sure you understand."

"Cool!" said Pearl eagerly. "What's on the menu?"

Christabel smiled. "We'll have samphire soup to start, I think, followed by sea grapes and arame biscuits," she said. "Then shredded sea palm with just a *touch* of pearl extract for dessert. How does that sound?"

Pearl clapped with excitement. But Gilly looked like she'd eaten a sea slug.

"Will you sign a sea grape for me, Christabel?" Mabel asked.

"You are SO weird," said Orla.

"FINE," Miss Tangle said, even though it plainly wasn't fine at all. "The rest of us will eat our lunch by the air fountain. Then we'll meet in the Great Shell Hall. No dawdling! We have a LOT to get through today!"

Chapter Five

Marnie was glad Barbela swam with them through the palace to the restaurant. Word had spread, and there were Christabel fans around every corner and lurking behind every door.

"I love you, Christabel!"

"Christabel's my favorite name!"

Barbela swelled up like a sea-serpent every time someone got too close, and waved her trident.

"It's the price of fame, darlings," Christabel explained as they sat at a restaurant table beside a huge crystal window with a view over the coral gardens, with Barbela keeping guard. "Would anyone like a sea grape?"

Marnie wasn't hungry. She'd only just eaten her seaweed wraps and sea-cucumber slices. And anyway, the other diners were watching them and it was making her uncomfortable. So she just looked around the grand restaurant with its pearl-studded statues and shell chandeliers, and gazed at the dessert trolley with its gleaming dishes of pearl extract. The lobster waiters whisked about, carrying bowls of pretty pale-green samphire soup high above their heads.

"I'm having the BEST time with you guys," Mabel said, helping herself to a cluster of sea grapes.

"You can hang out with us any time," said Pearl.

Mabel's eyes widened. "Really?"

"Sure," said Orla between mouthfuls of crispy arame biscuit.

"I don't know why Gilly is always so horrible to you," Mabel said. "You're all really nice." And then she blushed and sipped her samphire soup.

A lobster waiter scuttled over to their table. "Miss Blue," he said with a bow. "Will you do us the honor of singing?"

"Excuse me, darlings," Christabel said to Marnie and the others. "Duty calls."

She put down her soup spoon, swam toward the huge driftwood piano which stood beneath a crystal dome at the center of the restaurant. She spoke to the squid piano player, and then started singing 'Clamshell Heart.'

"You're so lucky to have Christabel as your aunt, Marnie," Mabel sighed, as Christabel sang and the squid played and the diners applauded.

"Do you think I can have Christabel's soup?" Orla said.

Christabel gave up a lot for her fans, Marnie thought. *Even her lunch.* She didn't think she'd enjoy being famous.

Marnie and her friends drifted out of the restaurant with Christabel and Barbela and made their way to the Great Shell Hall to join the others.

Everyone was sitting on coral benches, waiting for them. Mr. Kelp-Matthews had fallen asleep. Dr. Wetson was surrounded by scallop messengers again. Mr. Scampi and Lady Sealia were both staring at a large portrait of a merking with wild grey hair and a large trident. Dilys floated beside them, yawning.

"Nice of you to join us," said Miss Tangle sarcastically. "We are now running extremely late. I have held our group tour—"

"How kind!" interrupted Christabel. "However, we won't need the group tour, Miss Tangle. I met the most charming merman in the restaurant, who gave us tickets for a VIM—Very Important Mermaid—tour instead. I simply *couldn't* say no." She blushed a little, and fanned herself with the five gold-edged tickets.

"I'm sure you could have," said Miss Tangle stiffly. "If you tried."

"Saying no to one's fans is always a terrible mistake," said Christabel. "Without them, I am nothing. I only wish I could have arranged VIM tickets for you all."

"A VIM tour!" Mabel gasped.

"Does this mean we'll see stuff no one else can?" asked Orla.

"Like Queen Maretta's ultra-rare fish collection?" Pearl asked hopefully.

This was the first Marnie had heard about a VIM tour. Gilly glared at again. Marnie felt a blush creeping up her whole body, from the tip of her tail to the top of her head.

"So please go ahead without us," Christabel said. "And give my *deepest* apologies to the guide for keeping you all waiting."

Miss Tangle swelled up like a furious, ink-filled balloon. "Then we'll see you back at the whale shark at half past the afternoon starfish," she said. "And if you are late, we **WON'T WAIT**. You will have to make your own way home."

"Of course, Miss Tangle," said Christabel in a soothing voice.

"Come along then, everyone," Miss Tangle said shrilly. "We don't need VIM tickets! We're all going to have a marvelous time with Colin, who knows **EVERYTHING** about the palace!"

Colin, the tour guide, was a sad-looking electric eel in a hat. His tail shot out a couple of sparks as Christabel blew him a kiss. Miss Tangle made a Typhoon-ish noise, and ushered the rest of the group along with her tentacles.

Marnie felt someone barge into her shoulder.

"I bet you're really enjoying this," Gilly hissed. "Stealing my friend and lording it over everyone else. You think you're so much better than us, don't you?"

"What? No, I don't—" Marnie began, but Gilly had already swum away with a flick of her tail.

"You're very quiet, darling," said Christabel, as they passed through a large set of golden doors into the palace's famous Crystal Ballroom. "Is everything all right?"

Marnie didn't want to be ungrateful. Christabel had gone to so much trouble for the group, buying them lunch and getting them such a nice tour. They had gone to the front of the long line and everything. But she still felt weird.

"I'm not used to the high life, I guess," she said.

Christabel put an arm around Marnie. "Come on now. Don't be sad," she said. "It's fun to have this all to ourselves. Look at these chandeliers! They're almost as big as my best earrings."

Marnie gazed around the glittering Crystal Ballroom with its famous wall mirrors. Garbo swam from mirror to mirror, admiring herself.

"I heard there's a SUPER-rare goldflake angelfish in the Royal Collection," Pearl said. "Is it true?"

Their VIM guide—a handsome blond merman named Herman—scratched his golden beard. "I don't know about that," he said. "But the chandeliers are home to two thousand lampfish, which light the place up for parties."

"Lampfish are boring," Pearl said. "A goldflake angelfish is WAY more interesting. It can find gold anywhere. Isn't that amazing?"

"We should move on, Miss Blue," said Barbela, who was still guarding them with her trident. "A large party is approaching."

"What a shame," said Christabel with a sigh. "Lead on, Herman." She put her arm on Herman's shoulder. "Goodness, aren't you muscly? Like a lovely muscly mussel."

Herman grinned. "Thank you, Miss Blue. I'm a huge fan, by the way."

Christabel fluttered her eyelashes and laughed.

Marnie was surprised that her aunt was flirting with Herman. She thought about Arthur. She didn't know much about love, but she knew that you didn't usually flirt with other merfolk.

Orla linked arms with Marnie. "IMAGINE being at a ball in the Crystal Ballroom!" she said, twirling Marnie around. "The music, and the dancing, and the ballgowns—"

"What's that?" said Barbela suddenly.

"What's what?" said Orla.

Barbela frowned around at the empty ballroom. "I thought I saw someone," she said.

The Crystal Ballroom was completely empty.

"You said there's a big party coming," Mabel offered. "Maybe one of them is early."

Barbela frowned around the room one more time. "Maybe you're right," she said.

"Let's keep moving then," said Herman. "Follow me!"

"I would follow you anywhere, Herman," Christabel purred.

Marnie and the rest of the VIM party left the Crystal Ballroom through a small, mirrored door. It was tucked among the other mirrors so that it was nearly impossible to spot.

"Queen Maretta's secret exit," Herman said as they all swam through. "She was always the center of attention at the balls, and she used to get very tired of it."

"I know how she feels," said Christabel.

"She would slip away when no one was looking and visit her Jewel Room," Herman explained. "That's where we're going next."

They swam down a tall corridor with high crystal windows on either side. Through the windows, Marnie glimpsed the fantastical shapes of Queen Maretta's coral gardens and the brightly colored fish that darted among the coral branches.

"Green swordtail, red swordtail, orange butterfly fish," Pearl said, gazing out of the windows as they swam along.

"Why don't we have dinner some time?" Christabel suggested to Herman. "I think that we have LOTS in common. We both have tails, we're both good swimmers, and you have enough muscles for the both of us."

"I'd like that," Herman said.

Marnie tugged at her aunt's sleeve. "Aunt Christabel?"

"Hmm?" said Christabel.

"What about Arthur?" she said, in her lowest voice. *"Your boyfriend?"*

"Oh, Marnie!" Christabel exclaimed. "Arthur and I aren't together anymore."

Marnie's mouth fell open. "But he came to see you at the Clamshell Show!"

"And I sent him away," said Christabel. "Remember? Lady Sealia made it very clear that he could never return."

This wasn't what Marnie had expected. "But what about the crystal tears?" she said, feeling baffled. "What about your true love?"

Christabel took Marnie's hand. "Those crystal tears weren't mine, darling. They were Arthur's. I met him at the East Lagoon Rocks yesterday and gave them back to him. That's why I was late for dinner."

Marnie couldn't believe it. Everything she'd thought was wrong. "So Arthur loved you, but you didn't love him?" she said.

"Oh, I loved him," said Christabel with a sigh. "But I belong in the lagoon, darling. If I lived ashore with Arthur, I'd lose my tail. More importantly, I'd lose my voice. And I AM my voice. The water is my element, not the land. That can never change. Arthur understands that now."

"But I made a wish when I put on the Golden Glory Crown," Marnie stammered. "I wished for you to find happiness!"

"And I have!" Christabel said. "Since ending things with Arthur, a weight has been lifted off my shoulders. I can concentrate on my career, and you and your mom, and all the other things that make life so marvelous. Like Herman and his muscly shoulders."

Happiness is a slippery fish and swims where it wants. That's what Queen Maretta had said when Marnie made the wish. It looked like the mermaid queen was right.

"Well," Marnie said at last. "As long as you're happy."

"Happier than I've been in *years*, darling," Christabel assured her.

Marnie realized she still had a lot to learn about love and happiness. With a sigh, she put away her thoughts of wedding parties and tidesmaid dresses.

"What's that?" asked Mabel, pointing to a large, shell-encrusted door on their right.

"The entrance to Queen Maretta's maze," Herman said. "The Queen loved playing practical jokes on her guests. She would trick merfolk into entering the maze, and then swim off. There are rumors that some of her more unpleasant guests never came out again. There's a door at the far end that leads into the Jewel Room, if you know how to find it."

"Cool!" said Mabel. "Can we go in?"

Herman shook his head regretfully. "It's closed for maintenance."

Marnie felt another rush of disappointment. She'd wanted to see the maze.

"But this is a VIM tour," Orla said. "I thought we could go anywhere?"

"Not the maze," said Herman. "It's not safe for anyone, even VIMs. But don't worry! We are going to have an exclusive experience in the Jewel Room that you'll treasure forever."

They swam down a long twisting corridor full of bored-looking anglerfish, who switched on their lights as they passed and switched them off again as they left. Herman told them about the portraits on the walls of long-dead royal merfolk and family seahorses. Marnie felt as if they were swimming in a vast circle.

Finally they reached the Jewel Room. The room was large and dark, and the walls glowed with phosphorescent fish. Jewelry lay in tall crystal cabinets all around, sparkling and gleaming.

"Oh!" said Orla, transfixed by the glittering.

Mabel's mouth hung open. Even Pearl looked impressed.

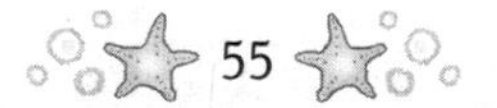

Christabel trailed her fingers over a large crystal display cabinet which held a magnificent golden tiara. "Exquisite," she said.

"Try it on," said Herman. "VIM tour guests are allowed to take the jewels out of their cases and try them on. Everything is open. Try on whatever you like." He wagged a finger. "Just don't steal anything. We will be checking!"

Marnie, Mabel, Orla, and Christabel flew to the display cases with delight. Orla draped herself in crystal

and mother-of-pearl. Mabel tried on an opal tiara that nestled in her dark hair beautifully. Christabel hummed as she clipped on a pair of glittering gold earrings. Garbo, who adored sparkly things, was so overcome that she spun around in the fastest circles Marnie had ever seen, causing tiny whirlpools above their heads.

"Aren't you going to try anything on, Pearl?" Marnie asked, trying on a beautiful gold and crystal necklace.

"I'd rather see a goldflake angelfish," Pearl admitted. She pressed her hand against a display cabinet full of gold rings. "It would love it in here."

"I am the Queen," said Orla, propping up the huge tiara on her head. She held up a giant crystal orb which glowed and shimmered. "Bow before me."

"That's the Ocean Orb of Truth," said Herman. "It shows the truth to anyone who looks into its crystal depths. But beware! If you've done anything bad, the Orb will know."

Marnie gasped. The actual Ocean Orb of Truth was in Orla's hands! Queen Maretta had used the Orb to find out the truth about all sorts of things—from courtiers telling lies to peace treaties that weren't going to be peaceful after all. Orla put the Orb down a little nervously.

"Time to put everything back anyway," said Herman, checking his starfish watch. "We still have the Royal Bedchamber, the Frozen Bathchamber, and the Sparkly Stables to see. The guards will lock up for us."

They reluctantly put the jewels back in the cases. Christabel made Garbo open her mouth and spit out a pair of crystal rings. Marnie gazed one last time at the Orb, glowing on its sea-moss cushion, and followed the others.

There was a sudden crash outside the doors. The guards rushed past Marnie and the others with their tridents raised. Everyone gazed in surprise at a jagged hole in the corridor window. A butterfly fish swam in, sniffed around, and then swam out again.

"Vandals," said Barbela with a sigh. "Throwing rocks and breaking windows so they can swim inside free of charge. Check it out, you two," she told the two Jewel Room guards. "We can't allow anyone into the palace without a ticket."

Marnie frowned. There wasn't any broken crystal on the corridor's sea-moss carpet. And if someone had thrown a rock from outside, then where was the rock?

A slight movement near the doors of the unguarded Jewel Room caught her eye. But when she looked, there was nobody there.

Chapter Seven

Marnie's tail was weary as they swam on, but she forgot about it when she saw the gift shop. There were model air fountains that blew real bubbles, seagrass notebooks stamped with Queen Maretta's initials, clam erasers, seahorse pencils, sea-silk scarves, crystal necklaces, Queen Maretta dolls, and driftwood rulers studded with tiny crystals.

There was no sign of the others. They must have already visited the gift shop. It was getting late, Marnie realized. The whale shark was going to leave soon.

"This is always the best part," said Orla happily, picking up a pen with a fluffy sea anemone on the end. "Although the Frozen Bathchamber was cool. That massive ice-block bath! Can you believe it never melts?"

"I liked the Sparkly Stables," said Mabel. She stroked a toy seahorse that lit up when you pressed its back.

"Do you sell model goldflake angelfish?" Pearl asked the merman behind the till, but he shook his head.

"Gifts for my group," Christabel said. "Pick out anything you like, my darlings."

Mabel picked up the toy seahorse and a large bag of fizzy whelks. "Even these?" she said hopefully.

"Even those," said Christabel.

Mabel squealed and swam around in circles, like Garbo had in the Jewel Room.

Orla picked up a polished black crystal and clutched it to her heart. "Thank you, Christabel," she said, beaming. "This whole day has been off the *reef*."

Marnie decided to spend her own sand dollars on a clam eraser. She swam over to the register. To her surprise, she caught a glimpse of golden hair whisking behind one of the shelves.

"Gilly?" she said. "What are you doing here?"

Gilly Seaflower swam sulkily into view, clutching her pearl backpack tightly to her chest. "I'm allowed here, same as you," she said. "You're not the boss, Marnie Blue."

"Have the others been to the gift shop already?" Marnie asked.

"How should I know?"

"You were with everyone else. Weren't you?"

Gilly pouted. "I wasn't going to let you steal my best friend and do loads of cool VIM stuff without me," she said. "I've been following you **ALL DAY** and no one even noticed. I would be an amazing catfish burglar," she added, a little thoughtfully.

Marnie suddenly understood. Those times on their tour when she'd thought someone else was nearby . . . It had been Gilly!

"What are you doing here, Gilly?" Orla demanded, swimming over. Mabel followed.

"I wanted to be with Mabel and Mabel wanted to be with me," Gilly said loudly. "We do EVERYTHING together. Don't we Mabel?"

Mabel looked uncomfortable. "You're supposed to be with Lady Sealia," she said. "She'll be worried if you aren't in her group."

"I don't care about Lady Sealia," said Gilly. She tried to link arms with Mabel.

"Don't do that," said Mabel. She pulled her arm away. "You ALWAYS do that. I've had a really nice time today and now you're ruining it. You can't just do whatever you want all the time."

Marnie couldn't believe her ears. Mabel *never* stood up to Gilly.

Gilly's mouth fell open. "But you're my *friend*!" she said furiously.

Mabel lifted her chin. "I am, but I can have other friends too."

"Yeah, and we like you, Mabel," said Orla. "Even if you are a bit weird about signing cookies."

Gilly's chin trembled.

"Come on," said Mabel. "You can buy something from the gift shop and we can go and find Lady Sealia together. She won't mind when we explain what happened."

Gilly's eyes filled with angry tears. "I don't need anything from this stupid gift shop," she said. "I've got something a MILLION times better." And she stormed out of the shop, past a very surprised Barbela.

"Do you think we should follow her?" said Marnie.

Mabel looked worried. "Maybe," she said.

"No way, stingray," said Orla. "Gilly is a pain in the tail. Why are you even friends with her, Mabel?"

Mabel shrugged. "We like the same stuff. Singing and performing. Gilly understands how important music is to me." She blushed. "Your aunt is the same, Marnie. That's why I love her so much."

Pearl swam over, clutching a little fish necklace. "They didn't have a model goldflake angelfish so Christabel got me this instead." She glanced at the doorway. "Was that Gilly? I thought she was in Lady Sealia's group."

Miss Tangle's face loomed in the gift shop window. She was pointing furiously at all the watches on her tentacles.

"I think Miss Tangle wants us to leave," said Christabel. She waved at the octopus. "We'll be out in a moment, Miss Tangle! Marnie, let's buy this scarf to cheer up your poor sick mother." She picked up a beautiful sea-silk scarf decorated with tiny seahorses.

After paying, they swam out of the shop. The others were gathered by the air fountain, with the whale shark parked and ready to go. Lady Sealia's seashell carriage looked a little dented.

Typhoon floated patiently in the harness. It looked like the morning's ride had tired him out.

"I have bought you ALL a little something," Christabel announced, sailing up to the whale shark with her scarf streaming behind her. "To show you how sorry I am that I couldn't get VIM tickets for everyone. You are *all* VIMs in my eyes." And she produced an enormous bag of fizzy whelks.

Everyone cheered. Marnie was suddenly surrounded by her friends, all munching fizzy whelks and asking how the VIM tour had gone. She told them about the Jewel Room and the Sparkly Stables, but left out the part about trying on the jewelry. She didn't want to sound like she was showing off.

"We had a good time too," said Lupita. "Allira stole Colin the tour guide's hat and hid it in a chandelier. Fresca and Ripley pretended to be statues so Mr. Scampi thought he'd lost them."

"Dr. Wetson had to resuscitate Salmonella after she swallowed too much air on the air fountain," Dora added. "Her burp was AMAZING, though."

Lupita giggled. "And Mr. Kelp-Matthews kept saying 'That Christine Blue girl should be on the radio. She's awfully good.'"

"Has anyone seen Gilly?" Marnie asked, looking around.

Cordelia Glitter ate another fizzy whelk. "Haven't seen Gilly all day," she mumbled. "She was supposed to be in our group, but Dilys got sick in the Coral Throne Room and Lady Sealia forgot to do a tail count."

There was a stir and a ripple in the water. Marnie saw twenty guards pouring out of the palace doors, led by Barbela.

"Can we help you?" said Lady Sealia, peering out of the seashell-carriage window as they were surrounded by shining tridents.

"I'm very sorry about this," said Barbela. "But it seems that the Ocean Orb of Truth has gone missing."

Marnie's eyes widened. The Orb was *missing*? But they'd just seen it on its cushion in the Jewel Room.

Barbela pointed her trident straight at Christabel.

"Miss Blue?" she said. "I would like you and your group to turn out your bags."

Chapter Eight

"Barbela, darling," said Christabel in astonishment. "What is this about?"

"You and your party were the only VIM tour in the palace today," said Barbela. She kept her trident pointing at Christabel. "The jewels were unlocked for you to try on. When the guards came to lock up again, the Orb was missing."

"That's got nothing to do with us," said Pearl. Her eyes were round and alarmed behind her glasses. "We're not thieves."

"I'm sorry, Miss, but facts are facts," Barbela said. "Turn out your bags, please."

Lupita looked at Marnie. "You never said you actually tried the jewels on," she said.

"A guilty conscience perhaps," Barbela said, eyeing Marnie.

Marnie felt flustered. "We put them back!" she said. "Honestly, we did."

"A likely story," snorted Barbela. "Bags, please!"

Marnie, Orla, Pearl, and Mabel floated together, blushing as the palace guards tipped their bags out on the seabed and sifted through seaweed hankies, hair bobbles, and half-empty sea anemone juice bottles. Marnie's clam eraser bounced away into a clump of seaweed.

"Your bag too please, Miss Blue," said Barbela.

"Be careful," Christabel said, passing Barbela her handbag. "It's by Valentuna."

"I'm sorry officers, but will this take much longer?" said Lady Sealia. "We have a long swim home, and Dilys needs her din-dins."

"The Orb is one of our most important artifacts, Madam," said Barbela, handing back Christabel's bag. "We must make every effort to find it. I'm going to have to take Miss Blue and her group for questioning. Follow me."

"But we are on a schedule—" began Miss Tangle.

"So are we, Miss," said Barbela.

Marnie and the others were herded back to the palace like a school of fish.

"Unbelievable," said Orla furiously as they were jostled along. "They can't do this!"

"They're guards with tridents," said Pearl. "They can do anything they want."

Marnie's brain was whirling. She was *sure* the Orb had been on its sea-moss cushion when they left the Jewel Room. Who could have—

"Gilly!" she gasped.

Pearl looked around. "Where?"

"Gilly has the Orb!" Marnie tried to keep her voice to a whisper. "She was following us . . . None of us took it, so it must have been her! When that window smashed, there was no rock or broken crystal inside the palace. Gilly must have thrown something OUT of the window instead, to distract the guards."

"It worked," Pearl said. "I've never seen two mermen swim so fast."

"Leaving the jewels unguarded!" Marnie said. "When Gilly said she had something better than the stuff in the gift shop? She was talking about the *Orb*."

"What was she thinking?" said Orla.

"She was just jealous that we did a VIM tour with her friend," said Marnie. "It's totally the kind of thing Gilly would do."

The others had to agree.

"But she could go to *jail*!" said Pearl.

Mabel looked anxious. "I don't want Gilly to go to jail. I know she's annoying, but she's my friend. I should have stayed with her like she wanted. Then none of this would have happened."

"It's not your fault, Mabel," said Marnie. "We have to find Gilly before the guards do."

"In case you hadn't noticed, we're surrounded by tridents," Pearl pointed out. "How are we going to get away?"

They were taken to a cave off the Great Shell Hall. The guards spread out to stop anyone else from leaving or entering the palace. One guard remained outside the cave. One followed them inside.

“We’re going to question you one at a time,” Barbela announced. “Miss Blue? As the responsible adult, I will start with you.”

“This is all a terrible misunderstanding,” said Christabel. She adjusted her sea-moss scarf. “But we will all do our best to help. Wait here, darlings,” she said to Marnie and the others.

Marnie, Orla, Pearl, and Mabel sat on a bench as Christabel and Barbela vanished into an office. They stared glumly at the guard leveling his trident at them. The guard stared back.

"Atchoo," Pearl began. "Atchoo. ATCHOOOO!"

Marnie realized the bench was made of coral.

"What's with the sneezing?" said the guard suspiciously. "I have a very delicate constitution. I can't be exposed to illness."

"My friend is allerg—" Orla began.

"ILL!" said Marnie suddenly. She'd had an idea. "She's really ill. And it's extremely infectious."

The guard floated back against the cave wall. His trident trembled.

Pearl's eyes were red and puffy now. "ATCHOOO!" she said.

"You had better get a doctor," Marnie told the guard. "My friend is EXTREMELY SICK. If she doesn't get some medicine, she might die. So will you," she added, as an afterthought.

The guard looked horrified. "If it's so infectious, how come you're all still alive?"

Marnie stared at her friends. *Help me out!* she wanted to say.

"We were vaccinated last week," Mabel said, joining in.

Pearl's face was bright red. Blotches were appearing on her cheeks.

"There, there, Pearl," said Orla. "The nice guard is going to go get a doctor and save your life."

The guard fumbled for the cave-door handle. "I'll be back in a minute," he blurted. "Stay there."

The moment he had gone, Marnie jumped up.

"This might be our only chance to find Gilly," she said. "We have to swim for it."

"What about—ATCHOO!—the guard outside the door?" Pearl asked.

Marnie pointed at another door on the far side of the cave. "We'll try that one instead."

They carefully opened the door and peered outside.

"Looks like the coast is clear," Orla said.

With a flash of tails, the four mermaids shot into the corridor.

"Where should we start looking?" Mabel asked as they swam. "The Jewel Room?"

"Why would Gilly go back to the scene of the crime?" Orla said.

"I bet she got scared when the alarm was raised," Pearl said. "She's probably hiding somewhere, tucked away where the guards won't think of looking."

"We'll spread out," Marnie said. "And search—"

"HEY!" said an angry voice.

It was the guard they thought had gone to get a doctor. He was floating in the doorway they'd just come through, pointing his trident at them.

"Swim," Marnie told the others, abandoning any thoughts of a plan. "Just SWIM!"

The chase began. Marnie led the way, dragging Pearl by the hand. Mabel was fast and soon shot ahead. Orla stayed close to Mabel's tail. Behind them, Marnie could hear shouting and the clanking of tridents.

They had a good head start, but Marnie had a feeling the guards knew the twisty palace corridors better than they did. Had they come this way on the VIM tour? She stared at the seahorse portraits and the sleepy anglerfish as they sped along, hoping to recognize something.

They tore up crystal tunnels and through big, looming rooms with coral chandeliers that set Pearl sneezing again. But the guards were getting closer!

"Gilly!" Marnie called, panting. "Gilly, where are you?"

"Gilly!" shouted the others. "Gilly! GILLY!"

A pain was starting to bloom in Marnie's side as they hurtled into a familiar-looking corridor lined with crystal windows. There was a shell-encrusted door set into the wall. Marnie realized they had reached the maze.

"Is someone crying?" Orla said, cocking her head.

Marnie found it difficult to hear anything over the pounding of her own heart. But behind the shell door,

someone was definitely sobbing. A funny feeling swept over her: part excitement, part fear.

"Gilly's in the maze," she said.

"It's like I said," Pearl pointed out. "She's tucked herself away. The guards won't go in the maze. It's supposed to be closed."

"We have to go inside and find her," said Marnie.

Mabel's eyes widened. "But we can't go in the maze. It's dangerous. Herman said—"

The shouting and clanking of tridents was closer than ever.

"Herman schmerman," said Orla. And she pushed open the door.

Chapter Nine

The maze was very dim. Dimmer even than the Jewel Room. The rocky walls loomed in the darkness, and it was hard to see much further than their own hands. Pearl's glasses gleamed with little sparks of light as a phosphorescent fish swam lazily past their noses.

The sobbing was louder in here.

"Gilly!" Mabel called. "We've come to find you! It's me, it's Mabel!"

"Mabel?" A fresh burst of weeping echoed towards them. "Oh Mabel, I'm in so much trouble!"

"We'll help you to put the Orb back," Marnie said, feeling her way along the wall.

"Why did you have to bring Marnie Blue, Mabel?" Gilly complained, sounding more like her normal self. Then her voice grew more cautious. "How do you know about the Orb?"

"It didn't take a brain sturgeon to figure it out," said Orla.

"Orla Finnegan's here? I suppose you've got that weirdo Pearl Cockle too."

"I'm not weird," said Pearl indignantly.

Orla squinted into the darkness. "If you're going to be mean, Gilly, we'll just tell the guards you're in here and they can come talk to you."

"Don't do that!" Gilly sounded frightened. "Don't leave me. I'm lost and I can't find the way out."

"Put your hand on the wall and keep turning left?" Mabel suggested.

"I already tried that," said Gilly with a sniff. "I just ended up in the same place. I know I'm going around in circles. I keep seeing the same stupid starfish clinging to the wall."

"What kind of starfish?" Pearl asked with interest.

"Not now, Pearl," said Marnie. "We have to get Gilly out."

"Why aren't there any anglerfish in here?" Orla said in frustration. "We can't see a thing."

"My toy seahorse," Mabel said suddenly. "It lights up!"

She pressed the button on her toy seahorse's back. The dark water around them began to glow as the seahorse turned all the colors of the rainbow: red, orange, yellow, green, blue, purple.

"I feel like I'm at a party," said Orla. "Good thinking, Mabel."

By the changing light of the seahorse, they could see three tunnels in front of them. The tunnels looked like the wide-open mouths of three enormous fish.

"Let's go," said Marnie.

"How are we going to find our way back?" said Pearl.

"I'll leave a trail of fizzy whelks," suggested Mabel.

Marnie swam into the first tunnel. The others followed cautiously. Every so often, Mabel dropped a fizzy whelk on the rocky ground.

"I hope the fish in here don't like sweets," said Orla.

Marnie hoped the same. But it was the best plan they had.

"Gilly!" she called. "Can you hear us? Can you swim towards our voices?"

"I . . . don't know. I can try maybe?"

Marnie stopped. A pile of rocks was blocking the way. The ceiling had caved in.

"Herman said the maze was dangerous," Mabel said, shivering. "What if more of the roof falls down while we're in the tunnels? We'll all be trapped."

Carefully, they swam back to the beginning and chose another tunnel, avoiding the rockfalls and calling Gilly as they went.

"Gilly! GIII-LLL-YYY!"

"I'm running out of whelks," Mabel said after awhile.

Gilly suddenly came hurtling around the corner. She flung herself at Mabel and hugged her tightly in the multicolored light.

"You came, Mabel!" she kept saying, over and over again. "I can't believe you came."

"We came too, you know," said Orla.

Gilly let go of Mabel and wiped her eyes. She looked at Marnie, Orla, and Pearl. "Thanks," she said, a little reluctantly. "I guess."

"Now all we have to do is follow the whelks out of here," Marnie said in triumph.

They all looked at the rocky ground.

"Um," said Pearl. "Where are the whelks?"

A tiny fish suddenly whisked past their tails. It was carrying a fizzy whelk in its mouth. They watched with dismay as it shot away through a crevice.

"You know that question about whether fish like sweets?" Orla said. "I think we just found out the answer."

They were deep inside Queen Maretta's maze now, with no way of retracing their route. To make things worse, Mabel's toy seahorse was starting to run out of batteries. Marnie tried not to panic in the dimming light.

"Any ideas?" she asked the others.

Gilly started crying again.

"On the VIM tour, Herman said there was a second door, that led from the maze straight into the Jewel Room," said Mabel. "Maybe we should try and find it?"

"But how?" said Orla.

Pearl made a peculiar noise. For a moment, Marnie thought she was choking on something.

"Goldflake angelfish," Pearl stuttered. "Goldflake angelfish coming this way!"

A neat fish with long golden fins swam around the corner. It stopped when it saw them. Its dark eyes grew wide. The mermaids stared at it.

"Nobody move," said Pearl urgently. "We don't want to frighten it."

"It's just a fish, Pearl—" Orla began.

"Mabel, do you have any more whelks?" Pearl interrupted. "Marnie, can I have your hair bobble?"

The goldflake angelfish was still watching them cautiously. Mabel thrust a fizzy whelk into Pearl's hand. Marnie untied her hair and handed over her pearl bobble.

"What are you going to do?" said Gilly with a sniff.

"I'm going to catch it," said Pearl. She held out the fizzy whelk and the hair bobble.

"I can't believe you're collecting fish right now, Pearl," said Orla. "Seriously, there is a time and a place."

"This fish is going to get us out of here, Orla," said Pearl. "Goldflake angelfish can find gold ANYWHERE. This guy is going to find the Jewel Room for us. Come on, little fish. I have a lovely fizzy whelk for you."

Slowly, the goldflake angelfish swam towards the fizzy whelk. As it opened its mouth and prepared to take a bite, Pearl looped Marnie's hair bobble around it and pulled tight. The fish froze with fright.

"Hold onto my tail, guys," Pearl said. "These little guys swim fast. Especially when they're frightened. WHOA!"

The seahorse toy blinked one last time and then went out. Marnie got her hand on Pearl's tail just in time. Mabel grabbed Marnie's tail, and Gilly grabbed Mabel's. Orla was the last in the chain, holding on to Gilly with all her might as the goldflake angelfish shot away in the darkness.

It was a strange sight: a chain of mermaids all holding tightly on to a small golden fish. They shot up dark passageways and down inky tunnels, through curtains of wet seaweed and, once, over a glowing squid with very large tentacles. The goldflake angelfish never paused for a moment.

"Are you sure we're swimming the right way?" shouted Marnie in the darkness.

"Just because it CAN find gold," said Orla, "doesn't mean that it will find gold RIGHT NOW."

Pearl sounded worried. "I didn't think of that."

"I feel sick," wept Gilly.

They swerved around a tight corner. Orla banged her tail into the wall and yelped. Marnie hoped Herman was right about another door. She hoped Pearl was right about the goldflake angelfish. She hoped a lot of things.

"*Ten goldflake angelfish, swimming really fast*," sang Pearl bravely.

"*Ten goldflake angelfish, swimming really fast*," the others sang back. "*And if* ONE *goldflake angelfish . . .*"

". . . *should find the door at last*," Marnie sang, gathering her courage.

". . . *there'll be*— OH!"

Pearl stopped. Marnie, Mabel, Gilly, and Orla all bumped into each other's tails.

"OW," said Gilly.

They were in a large chamber with a chandelier dangling above their heads. Lampfish darted around, throwing spots of light around the walls. Beneath the chandelier was a door with curly crystal handles. It was smaller and neater than the door they'd used to enter the maze. Mabel pushed down on a crystal handle. It was locked.

"Now what?" Gilly wailed.

Set into the wall beside the door was a strange-looking golden dial. The goldflake angelfish sniffed it eagerly.

"Gold," said Pearl in triumph. "See?"

Gently pushing the angelfish away, Marnie twisted the dial a couple of times. There was a click and a whir, but the door stayed shut. She ran her fingers over the eight little images set around the dial.

"They're pictures of fish," she said, frowning.

"Marlin," said Pearl, pointing to a graceful fish at the top of the dial. She pushed her glasses up her nose and looked a little closer. "Hammerhead. Angelfish. Ray. Eel—"

"I knew that one," interrupted Gilly.

"Squid, barracuda, and tuna," Pearl finished.

"It's a puzzle!" Mabel said with excitement. "I love puzzles. What do they have in common?"

"They're all fish," said Orla.

"Technically, a squid is a cephalopod," said Pearl. She was holding the goldflake angelfish again. It sounded like it was purring.

Mabel tapped her finger on her teeth, deep in thought. "It's probably about the names," she said. "What do they all start with?"

"M-H-A-R-E-S-B-T," said Marnie.

"That's not a word," said Gilly.

"Say something useful, or don't say anything at all, Gilly," Orla said.

"Maybe we should mix up the letters?" Pearl said.

R-S-T-E-M-B-H-A.

A-B-E-H-M-R-S-T.

R-T-E-M-S-H-A-B.

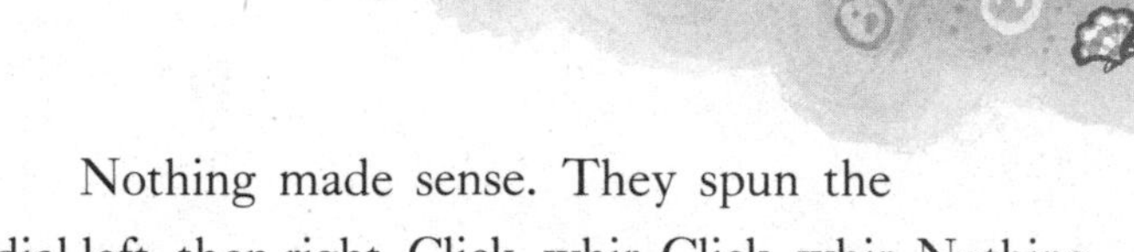

Nothing made sense. They spun the dial left, then right. Click, whir. Click, whir. Nothing.

"Maybe it's Maretta," said Gilly.

"We can't spell Maretta," said Orla crossly. "There's only one T and one A!"

Marnie felt a little flicker of hope. "That doesn't matter," she said. "M-A-R-E-T—we've got those letters. No one said we couldn't use the T and the A twice or that we have to use all the letters."

She twisted the dial carefully. M-A-R-E-T-T-A.

Click, whir . . . CLUNK. Suddenly, the door opened.

"Neptune's knickers," said Orla in astonishment. "Gilly did it!"

Gilly looked more surprised than anyone. The girls peeped into the familiar, glittering Jewel Room. There were two guards at the far end, beside the main door. But they hadn't noticed the second door or the mermaids peeking around the doorframe. Marnie put her fingers to her lips. She beckoned to Gilly.

"You have to put it back now," she whispered.

Gilly pouted. "I don't **WANT** to put it back."

"Don't be an idiot, Gilly," said Mabel. "It doesn't belong to you."

Gilly took the Orb out of her pearl backpack. She dropped her eyes to the glowing crystal ball in her hands. "I deserve nice things, the same as—**OH!**"

She gave a funny gasp. The guards looked around. Marnie pulled the door shut quickly. For a moment, they all waited for the guards to burst through and arrest them. But nothing happened.

"That was **WAY** too close," said Pearl.

"Do you **WANT** us to get caught?" Orla hissed.

Gilly had gone very pale. She shoved the Orb at Orla. "I don't want it now. Take it away."

Marnie remembered what Herman had said. *The Orb shows the truth to anyone who looks into its crystal depths. But beware! If you've done anything bad, the Orb will know* . . . She guessed that Gilly hadn't liked whatever she'd seen.

"You have to put it back," she told Gilly gently. "It's your responsibility."

"If you don't put it back, Gilly," said Mabel, "I won't be your friend anymore."

Gilly's eyes grew very wide. "OK, I'll do it," she whispered after a minute. "But what if I get caught?"

"Do we look like we care?" Orla said, folding her arms.

"We'll distract the guards," Marnie promised. "We'll swim out making tons of noise, so the guards chase us. Then you can put the Orb back and swim after us when the coast is clear."

Gilly held the Orb away from her. She gritted her teeth. Then she nodded at Marnie.

Marnie shoved open the door so that it flew back on its hinges with a CRASH.

"Come and get us!" she shouted at the startled guards.

The next few minutes passed in a blur. Marnie, Pearl, Orla, and Mabel swam around and about the crystal cabinets, whooping and yelling, beating the water with their tails so that it swirled and shimmered in the glittering, glowing light of the Jewel Room. The guards spun around, bumping into jewel cases, waving their tridents, and trying to figure out what was happening. Pearl released the goldflake angelfish, which shot straight at the guards and confused them even more.

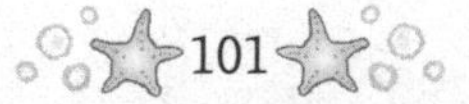

"Let's get out of here!" Marnie yelled, hoping Gilly had had time to put the Orb back.

They fled through the Jewel Room door and swam for their lives. Darting and diving, rolling and twisting, shooting high up towards the ceilings and low down so that their bellies grazed the sea-moss palace carpets.

The beaded bed-hangings in the Royal Bedchamber jingled as they passed. They plunged into the chill of the Frozen Bathchamber and dashed through the Sparkly Stables, making the seahorses snort and buck in surprise. Until finally—FINALLY—they made it to the courtyard.

They were free!

Marnie collapsed on the rocky edge of the fountain, clutching her chest. She could hardly breathe. Pearl, Orla, and Mabel barreled after her, almost crashing into the fountain itself. There was no sign of the whale shark or Lady Sealia's seashell carriage. It looked like the others were long gone.

"I did it!" Gilly shouted, flying out of the Sparkly Stables door a few moments later. "I put it back! And they already found it. I heard the guards talking about it when I was swimming through the Crystal Ballroom."

"I think we got away with it," Marnie said in wonder.

"Thanks to me," said Gilly with a toss of her long blonde curls. "I was so quick, you wouldn't believe it. AND I solved the puzzle on the dial."

"Aaand the old Gilly is back," said Orla.

"Maybe next time, don't steal any Crown Jewels in the first place?" Pearl suggested.

Gilly blushed. Mabel cheered. Orla lay back on the fountain in exhaustion and let the bubbles bounce her around for a bit.

"STOP!"

Marnie gasped as a line of guards swam toward the fountain. Orla jumped up so fast that the bubbles whooshed her almost as high as the palace roof. Marnie glimpsed the wafting sea-moss scarf of her aunt swimming among the gleaming tridents.

"You found the Orb, Barbela darling," Marnie heard Christabel say. "Surely that's the end of the matter?"

"This won't take long, Miss Blue." Marnie could see that Barbela was holding something carefully in her arms. "Just one look into the Orb and we'll all know what happened, won't we?"

Marnie swallowed. She should have known they wouldn't get away with something as serious as stealing one of the Crown Jewels—even if Gilly *had* put it back.

Gilly hid her face in Mabel's shoulder as the guards surrounded them again. Pearl had turned as white as the pearls around Orla's neck.

Barbela's glance was as sharp as a shark's tooth. The Orb glowed and swirled in her hands. "What a surprise to find the Orb safe and sound in the Jewel Room," she said. "My guards reported a strange disturbance involving four mermaids matching your descriptions. So I'm sure that you won't mind looking into the Orb for me now? Just to get to the bottom of the mystery. The Orb knows the truth about every bad thing you've done." She pointed at Pearl. "You first."

Pearl gazed into the glowing Orb. Her lip trembled. "I wasn't going to keep him," she burst out. The goldflake angelfish peeped out from under her school jumper. "He followed me and I couldn't make him go away! Am I in trouble?"

"We're not interested in the fish, Miss," Barbela said.

Pearl looked amazed. "But he's part of the Royal Collection," she said. "Isn't he?"

Barbela shook her head. "There hasn't been a fish collection in the palace for years. That's a wild one you've got there. You can keep him if you want."

Pearl sat down on the edge of the fountain, looking dazed. The angelfish darted happily through her long red hair.

Orla looked a bit sick as she stared into the Orb. "I didn't mean to break it, Sheela!" she said. Marnie hardly recognized her friend's voice. "It was an accident!"

Barbela peered over Orla's shoulder. "Just a personal matter," she told her guards. "Nothing for us to worry about."

To Marnie's surprise, Mabel lifted her chin and stared straight at Barbela. "I stole the Orb," she said. "You don't need me to look into it if I'm confessing, do you?"

"If it's all the same to you, Miss, I'd rather know the whole truth. We'll see for ourselves—"

"It wasn't Mabel."

Everyone looked at Gilly.

"It wasn't Mabel," Gilly muttered again. "Mabel is taking the blame for me. It's the nicest thing anyone has ever done for me in my whole entire life." She swallowed. "But please don't make me look in the Orb. I already looked once and it . . . it was horrible. I've done loads of bad things and I saw them ALL." She clasped her hands together and looked at Barbela. "Are you going to arrest me?"

Barbela leaned her trident against the fountain. "Taking one of the Crown Jewels is a serious offence, Miss."

"I know," Gilly whispered. "I'm really sorry."

"She did put it back," Marnie said. She felt a little relieved that she wouldn't have to look into the strange, swirling Orb.

"That's true, Barbela darling," said Christabel. "Let's all be friends now. I'll sign everyone's trident and you can put the Orb back and we can all go home."

Barbela considered. "Everyone's trident?" she said. "Even mine?"

Christabel produced a glittery shell pen from her Valentuna handbag. *To Barbela, the best guard in Mermaid Lagoon*, she wrote in lovely swirls and loops all down the trident handle. *Stay cool! Love, Christabel.*

The guards all started chattering with excitement.

"Could you sign my trident for my wife, Miss Blue?"

"Could you sign my shirt?"

Christabel signed everyone's tridents and shirts. She even signed Herman's muscly arm, with a little *Send me a scallop!* added at the end.

Barbela smiled goofily at her signed trident. Then she lifted it and pointed it at Gilly. Marnie held her breath.

"You're banned from the palace for life, Miss," Barbela said. "Let that be a lesson. Come along now, troops. We have a palace to protect."

The guards all waved their signed tridents and swam back to the palace. Marnie caught one last

glimpse of the glowing Orb in Barbela's arms, and it was gone. The palace doors swung shut, and they were alone in the courtyard again.

Gilly hugged Mabel. Orla hugged Marnie. Pearl hugged her angelfish. Garbo blew bubbles.

"What a day," said Christabel. She adjusted the sleeves on her jacket and patted her hair. "I've sent a nice little scallop to fetch us a shark taxi. Shark taxis are the fastest in the lagoon, and so elegant. We'll be home before you know it. Although I would advise you to keep your tails out of reach. It should be here shortly."

She grinned and paddled her long painted fingernails in the bubbling air fountain.

"Now," she said. "Who's up for a burping contest while we wait?"

What is Your Mermaid Name?

Find the month of your birthday and your favorite color to reveal your o-fish-al mermaid identity!

January	Coral
February	Delta
March	Shelly
April	Hallie
May	Nerissa
June	Andrina
July	Harmony
August	Lorelei
September	Marina
October	Serena
November	Cordelia
December	Melinda

Blue	Seagrass
Green	Kelp
Purple	Triton
Gold	Shore
White	Smallcove
Red	Fairweather
Pink	Waverly
Black	Tidesmith
Yellow	Fishmonger
Turquoise	Waters
Orange	Mangrove
Silver	Sandragon

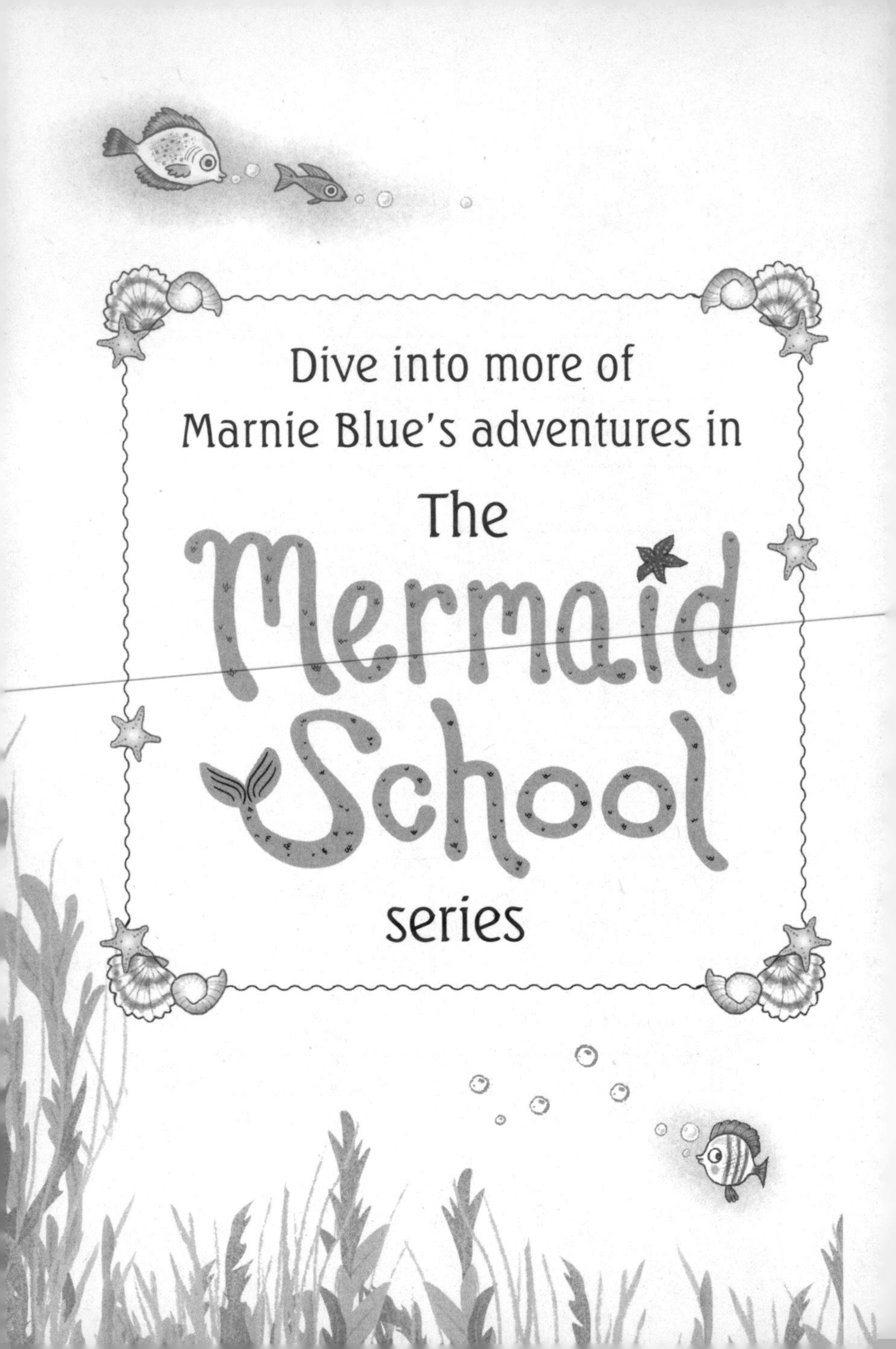
Dive into more of
Marnie Blue's adventures in
The
Mermaid
School
series

Mermaid School
Written By
Lucy Courtenay
Illustrated by
Sheena Dempsey
Mermaid School
The Clamshell Show
Written By
Lucy Courtenay
Illustrated by
Sheena Dempsey
Mermaid School
Ready, Steady, Swim!
Written by
Lucy Courtenay
Illustrated by
Sheena Dempsey
Mermaid School
Secrets of the Palace
Written by
Lucy Courtenay
Illustrated by
Sheena Dempsey

About the Author

Lucy Courtenay has worked on a number of series for young readers, as well as books for young adults. When not writing, she enjoys singing, reading, and traveling. She lives in Farnham, England, with her husband, her two sons, and a cat named Crumbles.

About the Illustrator

Sheena Dempsey is a children's book illustrator and author from Cork, Ireland, who was shortlisted for the Sainsbury's Book Award. She lives in London with her partner, Mick, and her retired racing greyhound, Sandy.